AESOP'S FABLES

retold by JOHN CECH

illustrated by MARTIN JARRIE

STERLING

New York / London

CONTENTS

THE FOX &
THE GRAPES

Fox was hungry. Fox was always hungry. One day as he was out looking for food, he saw some grapes hanging high up on a vine. The pickers had missed these when they had harvested the vineyard. The grapes were deep purple and looked delicious. Fox jumped for them. And he jumped. And he jumped again, as high as he could. But the grapes were just beyond his reach. As he slunk away, now tired and still hungry, he said, "I didn't want them anyway. I bet they were sour."

Just because something is out of reach doesn't mean it's bad.

THE ANT & THE GRASSHOPPER

I⊤ was the middle of winter, a frosty, clear day. Even though it was cold, Ant was basking in the sun, munching on some seeds from the great pile he had worked hard all summer to store away. As Ant was eating, Grasshopper came by, his stomach growling with hunger, and begged Ant for a seed or two.

"Well," asked Ant, "how did you spend your days this summer?"

"I went from leaf to leaf, nibbling and singing," replied Grasshopper.

"Didn't you put anything away for a time like this?" Ant asked.

Grasshopper shook his head sadly.

"Ah, Grasshopper," Ant said. He gave Grasshopper some seeds and sent him on his way with these words:

"If you don't work in the summer, you'll go hungry in the winter."

THE VAIN CROW

Crow thought he was very handsome. One day he found some beautiful, iridescent feathers that the peacocks and other birds had shed. Thinking they would make him look even better, Crow stuck a bunch of them in with his own tail feathers. Then he paraded around the meadow with a good deal of crowing and cawing to call attention to his new tail. The other birds laughed at him. "You look ridiculous," they cackled. "And besides, those are our feathers. We didn't say that you could have them!" So they surrounded Crow and plucked their plumes out of his tail and chased him away. Crow tried to pretend that nothing had happened, but he had learned:

Always be the bird that you truly are.

THE ROOSTER
& THE PEARL

ROOSTER was strutting his stuff in the barnyard one morning, hunting and pecking for breakfast, when he came across something round and shiny: a pearl. How it got there no one knows, but there it was, and Rooster thought it would surely be delicious. It looked like a very special seed. He pecked at it for a long time, but the pearl would not crack open. So he kicked the precious pearl into the straw and continued his search for something he could eat.

A jewel isn't a treasure to someone looking for a kernel of corn.

7

THE CITY MOUSE &
THE COUNTRY MOUSE

City mouse went to see his cousin in the country. It was quiet there, much too quiet for him, and he didn't like the food, either—just bread and cheese. Soon, City Mouse had had enough and said to Country Mouse, "Come to the city with me, and I'll show you how to really live!"

So, Country Mouse agreed to go to the city. When the cousins arrived at the grand house where City Mouse lived, they were very hungry from their trip. Inside, the mice found food left on the table in the dining room, and they helped themselves to cake and dabs of jam. Suddenly the hallway filled with barks and a huge snarling dog leaped into the room. The mice escaped by no more than a whisker.

"Don't worry," said City Mouse. "You'll get used to him. Isn't everything here so elegant?"

Country Mouse grabbed his pack and set off for home. City Mouse begged him to stay, but Country Mouse said, "No," thinking:

It's better to eat bread and cheese in safety than to run for dear life among delicacies.

8

THE DOG &
HIS SHADOW

DOG was having a great day. He had found a delicious bone and was going home to chew on it when he crossed a little bridge over a stream. As he looked into the water, he saw another dog who was holding a bone and looking back at him. *Hmmm,* Dog thought, *that dog's bone is bigger than mine.* And without thinking further, he made a grab for it. When he did this, the bone that Dog had fell into the water and was swept away.

If you reach for shadows, you're sure to lose what's real.

9

THE TORTOISE & THE HARE

EVERYONE knew that Hare was the fastest animal around, and Hare loved to brag about it. "I'm the fastest that ever was, is, or will be," he proclaimed. "Nobody can beat me!"

One hot day, Hare was bragging as usual and looking for a race when Tortoise walked slowly by and accepted Hare's challenge.

They asked Owl to be the starter: once around the park and back. Owl hooted, and they were off. Hare was soon halfway around the park, so he stopped to have lunch. Tortoise, far behind, kept slowly on.

With no sign of Tortoise, Hare had a nap. Tortoise just kept plodding on.

Hare napped all afternoon. When he woke up, he could see Tortoise in the distance, slowly heading for the finish line. Hare put on a burst of speed, zipping through the park to catch Tortoise. He was a blur of feet, his long ears stretched straight back. But he was too late. The winner was Tortoise—by a neck.

Keep a steady pace, and even the slow can win the race.

THE TWO CRABS

LITTLE CRAB was walking sideways across the sand, as he always did. Big Crab saw him walking this way and told him he was wrong. "You should be walking straight instead of sideways."

"But all crabs walk sideways," Little Crab said. "It's our nature."

"Not if they want to walk faster," Big Crab declared. All the while he was telling Little Crab what he should do, Big Crab was walking sideways himself.

"I'd be happy to walk straight ahead," Little Crab replied, "if you will show me how."

Sometimes people will give you advice about things they won't do themselves.

THE CROW &
THE PITCHER

It was hot, and crow was thirsty. He was in the middle of the desert, miles from anywhere. As he walked, he came across a pitcher with just a few drops of water in the bottom. But he couldn't reach his head and beak far enough into the pitcher to get the water. So he thought and he thought, and as the sun beat down, he got even thirstier. If he broke the pitcher, all the water would run into the sand. But if he couldn't get to the water, how could he make it come to him? Then he had an idea. He found a pebble and dropped it into the pitcher, and then another, and another. The more pebbles he dropped in, the higher up they pushed the water in the pitcher. Finally it was high enough for Crow to reach in and fill his beak. He drank enough to fly home, and as he flew he thought:

Good ideas are often the result of great need.

THE LION &
THE MOUSE

LION was sleeping one day when Mouse, who wasn't watching where he was going, ran over Lion's outstretched paw. Immediately, Lion woke up and trapped Mouse under his paw.

"What shall I do with you?" Lion asked Mouse.

"If you let me go," replied Mouse, "some day I will repay you."

The thought of Mouse doing him a good turn was amazing to Lion, and so he let Mouse go.

A few days later, Lion was captured by some hunters. They tied him up with rope so that they could move him the next day. That night, Mouse passed by again and saw the trouble that Lion was in. Mouse didn't need an invitation: he gnawed through the ropes with his sharp little teeth and set Lion free—just as he had promised.

Sometimes the smallest creature can be your biggest friend.

THE BEAR & THE TWO TRAVELERS

Two hikers were walking deep in the woods one day when an angry bear suddenly appeared out of nowhere. The bear stood on his back legs and roared. One of the hikers scrambled up a tree, while the other collapsed to the ground and pretended to be dead. He lay perfectly still, without breathing, and hoped the bear would leave him alone. The bear sniffed the hiker from his toes to his ear, and then walked away into the woods.

When the other hiker climbed down, he jokingly asked his friend, "What did the bear say to you?"

"Just this," replied the other hiker:

"When things get scary, a real friend won't run away."

THE FARMER & HIS SONS

A FARMER on the verge of death wished to make sure that his sons would pay proper attention to his farm, and so he told them that he had buried riches in one of his vineyards. The sons were eager to find the treasure, and started digging among the vines, turning over all the dirt and carefully sifting through it. They didn't find gold or jewels, but the grapes that grew in the vineyards the next year were the most delicious that anyone had ever tasted, and the sons became famous for their wine.

The reward for hard work is a treasure we can all find.

THE SUN &
THE WIND

SUN and Wind were arguing one day about who was stronger. Sun said, "I know how we can settle this. See that fellow walking down the road? Whoever can make him take his coat off first wins. I'll even hide behind those clouds and let you go first."

"Fine," said Wind, and he began to send his strongest gusts down on the man. He put on quite a show, sending trees crashing and bricks flying off chimneys. But the more Wind blew, the more tightly the man wrapped himself in his coat. Eventually Wind gave up, winded.

"Now, watch how it's done," said Sun as he came out from behind the cloud and slowly, calmly sent his rays streaming down on the man. Within a few minutes the man warmed up and happily took off his coat. He draped it over his arm, and smiled as he continued on his way.

Kindness and gentle warmth will always win out over harsh winds.

THE DOG & HIS MASTER

A BLACKSMITH had a dog that dozed all day while his master pounded away at his forge. As soon as the blacksmith sat down for supper, though, the dog would appear and beg for a part of the blacksmith's meal, even though he had already gulped down the food that the blacksmith had left for him. "I'll be happy to give you more," the blacksmith said, "when you learn how to help."

The most should go to those who work the hardest.

THE BUNDLE OF STICKS

A FATHER was worried about his sons. They were always quarreling, and were never willing to work together. One night the father showed his sons a thick bundle of sticks that he had tied together.

"Can any of you break this bundle?" he asked.

Each of the sons declared that he could since he was the strongest. But none of the sons were able to break the bundle, no matter how hard they tried.

Then the father untied the bundle. He put a stick into each of his sons' hands and asked each of them to break the single stick. This they were able to do easily.

"You see," the father said:

"Work together and you'll be stronger."

Dog was not the most civilized of creatures. Sometimes he would sneak up behind people and nip at their heels. To let people know Dog was coming, Dog's owner tied a bell to his collar. When Dog still kept nipping, his owner tied a wooden shoe to the collar to slow Dog down and give people a chance to get out of the way. Dog regarded these as splendid gifts. "No one but me has anything like this," Dog said as he showed off his bell and shoe.

"You're right about that," a wise dog said. "But I wouldn't be so proud of your collar if I were you," he said. *After all,* he thought:

A noisy reputation isn't necessarily a good one.

THE TREE &
THE REED

TREE thought he was the strongest thing on the river. "Look at my branches," he told a thin little reed that had planted itself nearby. "And look at my roots," Tree continued. "You should try to be more like me."

Reed replied, "I'm quite happy this way. I bend with the wind. I don't split or crack. I don't need more branches or deeper roots. The way I am is really just fine."

"Suit yourself," said Tree. "But one day you'll see I'm right."

The next week there was a terrible storm. It uprooted the tree and tossed it to the ground. Reed just bent with the gusts of wind, and when the storm was over, Reed straightened itself up again, good as new. And so Tree found out:

It's important to be able to bend when the storm arrives.

THE CAT &
THE MICE

THE mice were upset and held a meeting. The subject: how to deal with the cat that was forever sneaking up on them. They all agreed that the best thing to do was to tie a bell around the neck of the cat. That way, they could tell when the cat was coming and get out of the way. Ah, but then came a second problem: who would tie the bell around the cat's neck? Although all agreed it was an excellent idea, no one ever volunteered.

Don't propose what you won't do.

THE LION &
THE GOAT

Lion and Goat found themselves at the same small pool of water one hot summer day. Each one wanted to drink first, and each was too stubborn to let the other go first. Goat and Lion were on the verge of fighting when they noticed a group of buzzards in the tree above them, ready to help themselves to what was left of the loser. So Lion and Goat decided to stop quarreling and drink together and let the buzzards go find another meal.

Friendship—not fighting—fends off trouble.

THE MOUSE &
THE WEASEL

A LEAN and very hungry mouse one day found a basket full of corn with a hole in it. He easily squeezed through the hole and stuffed himself with corn until he could barely budge. When he was ready to leave the basket, he found that he'd filled out so much he could no longer fit through the hole.

Weasel was watching Mouse struggle and laughed at his predicament.

"What's so funny?" said Mouse.

"After all your eating, it seems that you'll have to stay in the basket until you've shrunk back to the size you were when you crawled through that hole."

Take just enough, and you won't get stuck.

23

THE BOY & THE HAZELNUTS

A BOY came across a jar of hazelnuts and couldn't resist, so he put his whole hand into the jar. He filled his hand with nuts, but then couldn't get his hand out again. He didn't want to let go of any of the hazelnuts, but he didn't want to leave his hand in the jar, either. He was stuck in this dilemma until his brother helped him sort it out:

Take a little at a time and you'll end up with a handful in the end.

THE BIG FISH & THE LITTLE FISH

A FISHERMAN drew in his nets, and all kinds of fish were caught. Big fish and medium fish, yellow fish and silver fish. But the little fish slipped through the web of strings that made up the net and swam away for another day.

Being small can sometimes be a very good thing.

THE MISER &
HIS MONEY

ONCE there was a miser who buried his money in a box in his garden. Each week he came to visit his money. He dug it up, opened the box, and counted his coins, laughing about how much he had. Then he put the money back into the box and buried it again.

One day, a passerby overheard him laughing. After the miser left, the stranger dug up the money and took it. The next time the miser came to visit his money, it was gone. He burst into tears and threw himself on the ground. His neighbors came to see what was wrong and he told them, between sobs, what had happened.

"What were you planning to do with the money?" one of the neighbors asked.

"Nothing," the miser replied. "I just wanted to look at it."

"Well, then, it doesn't matter that it's gone," said the neighbor. "It will do just as much good now as it did before."

If you don't use it, you may as well not have it.

THE ANT &
THE DOVE

ONE day Ant fell into the river. Dove, who saw him tumble in, plucked a leaf from the branch she was sitting on and dropped it onto the water next to Ant. Ant climbed on board and, although he was soaked through and through, managed to float to shore and safety.

Later Ant noticed a bird catcher preparing to spread glue on the branches where birds might land. Ant knew what the stranger was up to, and so he bit the bird catcher on the foot. The bird catcher howled in pain, dropped his glue bucket, and hopped out of sight. Meanwhile, Dove heard the noise and flew to a safe, high branch of the tree.

The best way to repay a good deed is to do one in return.

THE LADY & HER MAIDS

A LADY wanted her house cleaned every day, and so she employed two young women to work for her. The young women woke at dawn each day when the rooster crowed in the yard outside.

"I hate that rooster," one of the young women said. "Let's open the gate, and maybe the rooster will leave. Once it's gone, we can sleep later." Her friend agreed and they shooed the rooster out the gate. But in doing so, the young women found that their troubles only grew. Without the rooster crowing, the lady of the house didn't know what time it was, and so she roused the young women long before first light and set them to work.

If you try to cut corners, you may end up harming yourself instead.

THE SHEPHERD BOY & THE WOLF

WOLF was chasing a shepherd boy and had almost caught him when the boy turned to Wolf and said, "I know you've caught me, but please do one last thing for me."

"What's that?" replied Wolf

"Will you play a song on your pipe for me? Just a few notes, please?"

"All right," said Wolf, who cleared his throat and began to play. The shepherd boy started to dance, and so Wolf kept playing. Before he could finish the song, he heard the shepherd's dogs barking. They were getting closer with every bark. As he turned to escape, Wolf said to the boy, "Now that's using your head." Wolf should have known:

A wolf can't be a wolf and a piper, too.

THE BOY WHO WENT SWIMMING

A BOY swimming in the river went out too far. He tried to get back to shore, but he was tired and was just managing to keep himself afloat. Suddenly he saw someone walking along the shore and called to the man, "Help me! Help me, please!"

"Well, I'm not surprised you're in such a pickle," the man yelled to the boy. "You should know better than to drift out like that."

"Please!" the boy yelled back, "help me first and scold me when I'm back on shore!"

When someone needs help, actions are what really matter.

THE HEDGE & THE VINEYARD

WHEN his father died, a young man inherited his large estate, which included a sturdy border of hedges that ran along the outside of the vineyards on the property. But because the hedges didn't have any grapes on them, the young man tore them all out. It didn't take long before both animals and passersby helped themselves to all the grapes and the young man was left with none. And so he learned:

Carefully protect what's yours or others are sure to make it theirs.

THE BALD KNIGHT

A NOBLE knight who had lost his hair wore a wig so he wouldn't be embarrassed. One day when he was out riding with his friends, the wind blew off his hat, and then blew off his wig. All of his friends laughed, but the knight laughed loudest of all, because he had learned:

Always tell the bald truth, and then you won't need a disguise.

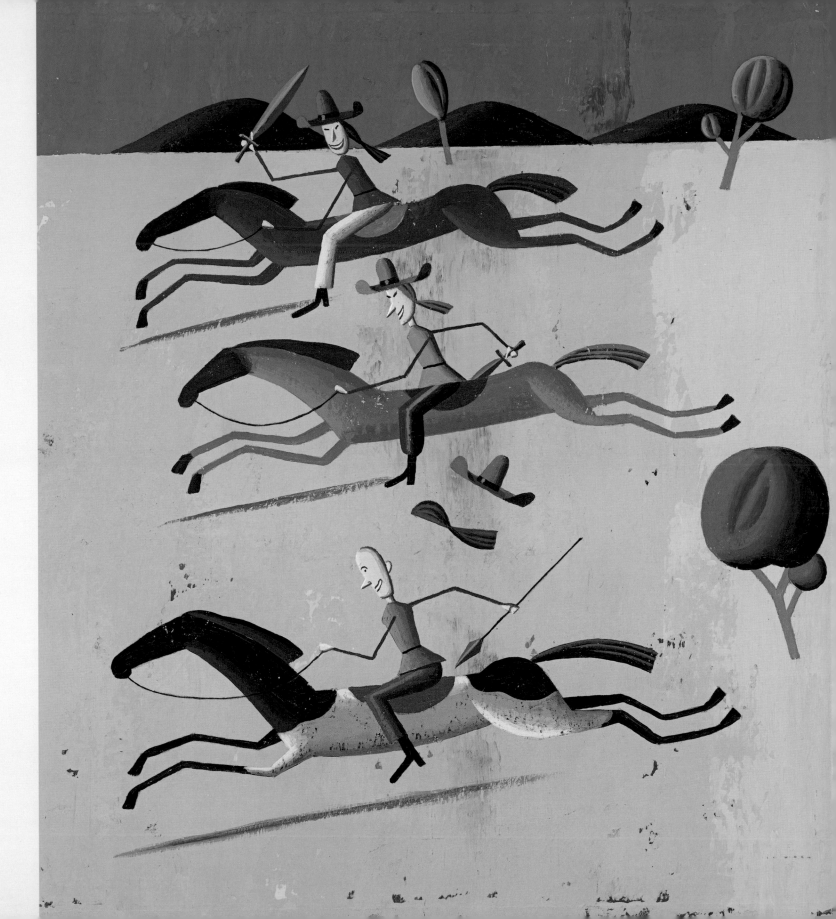

THE MILKMAID'S
MILKPOT

A MILKMAID thought aloud one day as she carried a large jug of milk on her shoulder from the barn to the house. "Suppose I were to sell this milk. With what I got I could buy a hundred eggs. And suppose I let the eggs hatch—that would be a hundred chickens. Now suppose I fatten up the chickens and sell them at the market. With the money I'll buy the finest dress that I can find, and wear it to the next dance. The young men will fall all over themselves asking me to dance with them. I'll look from one to the other like this . . ."

And as she practiced how she would look at the young men, she forgot all about the jug she was carrying. It slipped off her shoulder and crashed to the ground, taking her plans with it.

It's fine to make plans, but you must get the milk home first.

33

THE DOG IN
THE MANGER

IT was a chilly day, and Dog found a nice, comfortable, warm manger full of fresh straw to take a nap in. This was Ox's manger, and he came back to it in the evening to have his supper. Dog thought it would be fun to show Ox who was boss. So each time Ox tried to get close to the manger, Dog growled and snapped and chased him away. Despite his size, Ox was a peaceful creature, and in the end he simply ambled away to find hay somewhere else in the barn, thinking to himself how strange it was that . . .

Some will make trouble over things they don't care about.

THE SHEPHERD BOY

A BOY was tending a flock of sheep in a lonely valley. He was bored, and thought about how he could get someone to keep him company. Deciding on a plan, he ran into town crying, "Wolf! Wolf!"

A group of townspeople went back to the sheep with him, and several even stayed on for a few days just to make sure everything was fine with the flock.

Soon after they left, the boy did the same thing, and once again people from the town came back with him. But they could find no trace of a wolf—not even a paw print.

"Something's not right about this," one fellow said. And so the next time the boy ran into town crying, "Wolf! Wolf!" the townspeople went about their business.

"There really is a wolf this time," said the boy, but no one would believe him. And so the wolf helped itself to the flock of sheep.

"Why didn't you come when I called?" the boy later asked the townspeople.

"Ah, easy," someone replied.

If you tell lies, no one will believe your truths.

35

THE MONKEY
& THE CAMEL

AT a party in the jungle, Monkey did his famous dance. All the animals thought he was great and cheered for him. Camel wanted some of the applause, too, so he tried to dance just like Monkey did. But the animals all thought he looked ridiculous, and they yelled at him to stop trying to be like Monkey.

If you dance your own dance, you'll never be out of step.

THE FOX &
THE STORK

Fox and Stork were friends, or so it seemed until the day when Fox invited Stork for dinner. The dinner was soup, and Fox presented it to Stork in a dish. Poor Stork could only dip her bill in the dish, while Fox helped himself to his soup with his long tongue. "I'm so sorry you didn't like the soup," Fox said innocently.

"Never mind," said Stork. "Let me return the favor. Please come for dinner at my house tomorrow."

The next day, Fox appeared, hungry as usual.

Stork had prepared delicious soup, and served it to Fox in long, slender-necked jars. Poor Fox. His snout was too big to fit into the jars, and so he had to settle for the aroma of the soup.

As Fox left, Stork thought:

What goes around comes around—that goes for good deeds and for jokes, too.

THE ASTRONOMER

ONCE there was an old astronomer. He was always gazing up at the stars, even when he was walking outdoors. One day as he was strolling outside and looking through his telescope, he fell into a well. He cried out and his neighbor came to his rescue. As the neighbor pulled him out of the well, soaking wet, he said:

"If you keep your eyes on the stars, you'll miss what's on the ground."

THE SEA &
THE SHEPHERD

SHEPHERD loved the sea. Whenever he could, he drove his flock there and let his sheep nibble on the grass while he gazed out on the smooth waves. One day he decided that he would go to sea, and so he sold off his entire flock and bought a boat. He filled the boat with fruit, which he planned to sell on a nearby island.

On the way, a terrible storm broke the shepherd's boat to splinters and the fruit sank to the bottom of the sea. The shepherd barely escaped with his life. He went back to being a shepherd, and from then on whenever he heard anybody admiring the sea and how smooth it was and what a joy it would be to sail upon it, the shepherd always recalled:

A calm sea is just waiting for a trusting soul to sail upon it.

A NOTE ON AESOP

THOUGH MANY OF THE STORIES THAT WE CALL AESOP'S FABLES ARE FAMILIAR TO listeners around the world, we know very little about the person whose name is attached to these stories. One version of the story of Aesop is that he was a slave from Ethiopia (his name, some think, is derived from the name of the country and was used to describe, generically, a dark-skinned person). Aesop lived and created his stories around 500 BC on the island of Samos in ancient Greece.

Somehow Aesop won his freedom—perhaps because of his abilities as a storyteller— and he achieved some measure of fame for the ability of his tales to tell a story and make a point with economy, common sense, and sharp wit. Statues were created in honor of Aesop, one in Rome and one in Athens, and he is mentioned in the works of the Greek historian Herodotus, by the dramatist Aristophanes, and by the philosophers Plato and Aristotle. The first collection of Aesop's tales was not written down until around 300 BC, centuries after his death. One of the earliest books to be printed in English, by William Caxton in 1484, was a collection of Aesop's Fables.

Aesop himself told his stories orally, in the ancient tradition of the storyteller in societies that generally did not yet read and write. (The word "fable," in fact, comes from an ancient word meaning "to speak.") In these cultures, storytellers were among the most important people in the community. They knew a people's history, their myths and legends, their lore, and their shared experiences. Storytellers knew how to shape language beautifully and in ways that would hold a listener's attention. Most importantly, they knew a people's values, their strengths, their weaknesses, and their yearnings. These storytellers knew what made people laugh and what made them think.

Fables were, from their beginning thousands of years ago, stories about real, ordinary people. They were tales to be told in the fields and after supper or while traveling to market or the next village. These stories were about the consequences of our actions, foolish or careful, generous or greedy, cruel or kind. They were also about our destinies as human beings, at critical moments when we are able to make, in an everyday situation, a simple choice that could change our lives.

Many fables may be about animals, but they are really about human nature. And they were, and still are, about the lessons of life that we can learn if we simply and fully pay attention.

-J.C.

STERLING and the distinctive Sterling logo are registered trademarks of Sterling Publishing Co., Inc.

Library of Congress Cataloging-in-Publication Data Available

10 9 8 7 6 5 4 3 2 1

Published by Sterling Publishing Co., Inc.
387 Park Avenue South, New York, NY 10016
Text © 2009 by John Cech
Illustrations © 2009 by Martin Jarrie
Distributed in Canada by Sterling Publishing
c/o Canadian Manda Group, 165 Dufferin Street
Toronto, Ontario, Canada M6K 3H6
Distributed in the United Kingdom by GMC Distribution Services
Castle Place, 166 High Street, Lewes, East Sussex, England BN7 1XU
Distributed in Australia by Capricorn Link (Australia) Pty. Ltd.
P.O. Box 704, Windsor, NSW 2756, Australia

Printed in China
All rights reserved

The artwork was prepared using acrylic paint on paper.
Book design by Joshua Moore of beardandglasses.com

Sterling ISBN 978-1-4027-5298-8

For information about custom editions, special sales, premium and corporate purchases, please contact Sterling Special Sales Department at 800-805-5489 or specialsales@sterlingpublishing.com.